JAKE AND BO
MAGICAL CHR

ANN HATTAN

Illustrations by Jingo M. de la Rosa

AuthorHouse™
1663 Liberty Drive
Bloomington, IN 47403
www.authorhouse.com
Phone: 1-800-839-8640

Published by AuthorHouse 10/02/2012

ISBN: 978-1-4772-2748-0 (sc)
978-1-4772-2749-7 (e)

authorHOUSE®

It was the night before Christmas. Jake and his brother Zak were getting very excited about Santa coming.

“Come on boys, it is time for bed,” said their mummy, “but before you go, hang up your stockings and don’t forget to leave a mince pie for Santa.”

“I wonder what I will get tomorrow,” Jake said to his mummy.

“Well Jake, if you have been a good boy, you will get lots of nice things to open, so off you go to bed.”

“I love Christmas Mummy. It’s really lovely with all the decorations and the Christmas tree and lights. I wish it was Christmas every day!” Jake quickly undressed and went to bed. Before he got into bed he looked out of the window and watched the snow as it fell gently onto the ground. Looking up to the sky, Jake noticed a bright shining star. *What a beautiful sight,* Jake thought. He was delighted that it was snowing and said out loud, “Please Santa, will you bring me a cuddly rabbit and a sledge so that I can play in the snow tomorrow?”

Early the next day the boys awoke with great excitement, opening their presents as fast as they could. Jake noticed one particular present that was wrapped in bright red Christmas paper and had a large silver bow on it. *Could this be the cuddly rabbit that I have always wanted?* thought Jake as he opened the present. “What has Santa brought you, Zak?

“Lots of things--a train set, books and a cuddly elephant. What have you been given, Jake?”

“Just what I wanted; a cuddly rabbit, a sledge and lots of other things, too. I am going to call my rabbit Bobby.” Bobby was a grey and white fluffy rabbit with long floppy ears. Jake loved him as soon as he saw him. “We are going to have lots of adventures together,” Jake whispered to his new best friend. Jake was so excited with his new toy and went running into his parents’ room shouting, “Mummy, Daddy, Santa has brought me the rabbit that I wanted and I am going to call him Bobby.

“Do go back to bed, Jake. It is only half past six; it is not time to get up yet,” replied his mummy.

As soon as Jake and Zak got up, they asked if they could go out to play in the snow later on. “Yes, as long as you get wrapped up because it is very cold outside,” replied his mummy. They quickly put on their coats, hats and brightly coloured Wellington boots and out they went.

“The snow is very deep, Zak; it nearly comes up to my knees,” shouted Jake.

“This is fun,” replied Zak. “Please, can I have a go on your sledge?

“Yes, as long as you do not forget Bobby.”

“I will pull you along the snow.” When Zak had finished playing with the sledge he said, “Let’s build a snowman now, Jake.”

Both Jake and Zak quickly rolled all the snow into a large snowball and started to build the snowman. “I will go and get a hat and scarf,” shouted Zak.

“I will get a carrot for his nose, pebbles for his eyes and mouth and some buttons for his coat,” replied Jake.

“We also need some sticks for his arms,” shouted Zak. When they had finished building the snowman, both the boys thought how grand he looked.

“Shall we call the snowman Snowy?” asked Jake.

“Yes,” replied Zak.

“Come on in now!” called their mummy. “It is time for your dinner!”

“Are we having Turkey and Christmas pudding mummy?” shouted Zak.

“Yes” replied his mummy.

As the boys took off their wet clothes, their mummy asked if they had enjoyed themselves playing in the snow. “It was great,” replied Jake. “We had lots of snowball fights and we have built a snowman and called him Snowy. Come outside, mummy, and look at him,” Jake said.

“He is very grand,” said their mummy. After their dinner Jake and Zak started to play with all their other new toys until it was time for bed. “Come on Bobby, let’s go to bed now, as it’s getting very dark outside” said Jake. “What a fabulous day it has been” he said to his mummy.

After having been read a bedtime story, both the boys got into bed. Jake cuddled up to his new best friend Bobby and went to sleep. Suddenly Jake opened his eyes and noticed that Bobby was moving. Bobby looked at Jake and whispered, “Come on Jake, I am going to take you on an adventure.”

Jake was too shocked to speak but quickly put on his Wellington boots and coat and followed Bobby. “Where are we going?” he asked a few moments later.

“Come on!” Bobby replied. “I will show you.” Bobby quickly hopped down the stairs and out into the snow, followed closely by Jake. Once in the garden, he hopped toward the big oak tree and then stopped, looking behind him to make sure that Jake was still there.

"Bobby, where are we going?" asked Jake again. "We are going to see where Santa lives. He lives in Lapland, where everything is very magical," replied Bobby. When they approached the snowman that Jake and Zak had built earlier, Bobby stopped.

"Why are you stopping here?" asked Jake.

"We are nearly there Jake, come along," Bobby replied. Jake was very puzzled, but then he noticed something that had not been there earlier when he had built the snowman. *What is this?* thought Jake to himself. *There is a door in the middle of my snowman. I did not put a door there!* Bobby looked toward Jake and said "open the door Jake". Jake was afraid to open the door because he did not know where it would lead them. Somewhat nervously, Jake slowly opened the door and found that he was entering into a tunnel.

The tunnel was very dark, narrow and cold, with icicles hanging from the ceiling. Jake was starting to get very scared until he suddenly saw a light in the distance. "Look! We are reaching the end of the tunnel. It will not be long now until we are there," reassured Bobby. As promised, before long they reached the end of the tunnel. It was a magnificent sight. They were in a wood and all the trees were covered in snow, glistening in the sun. Bobby and Jake walked quickly through the wood and then in the distance Jake noticed that on top of the hill was a huge igloo.

"Are we going to the igloo?" asked Jake.

"Yes," replied Bobby, "but be warned, before we can enter the igloo there are some obstacles that we will have to overcome."

"What sort of obstacles?" asked Jake.

"Wait and see," Bobby replied mysteriously.

On they walked through the wood, which was curiously quiet. Jake was a bit frightened and kept looking behind him to check that nothing was following them. Walking through the wood, Jake saw a little igloo village in the distance. When they approached the village, Jake noticed that all the igloos were very small and he turned to Bobby and asked, "Who lives here?"

Bobby replied, "The elves, of course! They all work very hard, especially the few weeks before Christmas. They help to make all the toys for Santa!"

On Bobby and Jake went when all of a sudden Bobby shouted, "Watch out Jake, there is a large snowball with icicles sticking out of it rolling down the hill!"

Jake started to run as fast as he could so that the snowball did not knock him down.

"You have to keep a watch out for those huge snowballs, as they are very dangerous," called Bobby, "and do not forget to look out for the polar bears as well."

"How much farther do we have to go?"" asked Jake.

"Not too far now; we are nearly at the top of the hill," replied Bobby.

Just as they approached the igloo, Jake felt that there was someone following him. He quickly looked round and sure enough, there were two large polar bears behind him. Jake started to panic and ran as fast as he could and hid behind one of the tall trees. Fortunately for Jake, the polar bears did not see him hiding and ran straight on. *That was a narrow escape,* Jake thought to himself.

On they went until they came to the igloo. “Come on Jake,” shouted Bobby. “We are here.”

Jake was surprised when he reached the igloo. “It is so big!” he exclaimed.

Slowly they climbed up the steps until they came to the door. “Do you think Santa will be in?” asked Jake. “Of course, he will be relaxing now that he has delivered all the children’s toys.”

Once again Jake looked over his shoulder to make sure that the polar bears were not behind him and knocked on the door. “Do you think Santa will open the door Bobby?” Jake asked.

“I hope so,” replied Bobby.

Then all of a sudden Jake could hear footsteps and he knew someone was coming to open the door. As the door slowly opened, Jake started to get excited at the thought of seeing Santa. “Hello, you must be Jake,” said Santa as he opened the door.

“How did you know my name?” replied Jake.

“I know everyone’s name and I also know if you have been good,” said Santa. Santa was a jolly person with a big white beard. Jake was delighted that it was him who had answered the door.

Jake looked up at Santa and said, “Santa, where is your red coat?”

“I only wear that on Christmas Eve, as it is a magical coat,” replied Santa.

Slowly, Jake and Bobby followed Santa into his home. Santa took them into a very cosy room with a roaring fire, and Jake noticed that on the table beside Santa’s chair was a large red book with his name on it. Jake asked Santa, “Is that book about me?”

"Yes," replied Santa. "Would you like to have a look?"

"Yes please." As Jake opened the book, he was surprised to see that Santa knew all about him, where he lived and if he had been naughty or nice. Santa turned round, looked at Jake and said "You see, Jake, if you have been good most of the time, you will get extra toys and gifts at Christmas."

"Where are all the reindeer, Santa?"

"Come with me and I will show you."

Jake and Bobby followed Santa outside to the stable. As they walked around the back of his home, they could see hundreds of lights, glowing from the village of igloos. "Here they are!" said Santa.

"Do the reindeers fly?" asked Jake.

"Only on Christmas Eve," replied Santa.

In front of Jake and Bobby towered nine beautiful reindeer, all with shining coats of fur. They all had perfect antlers and hooves, as well. One reindeer, however, stood out from the rest.

"Who is this?" questioned Jake. "This is my most reliable reindeer, Rudolph." Jake could see that Rudolph had an amazing shiny red nose, which even glowed. Jake and Bobby patted the reindeer and fed them carrots before deciding to leave.

As they left the stable Bobby noticed that it seemed to be getting a little warmer and shouted, "Jake, I think we should be getting back because if the snow starts to thaw the snowman will have disappeared and we will not be able to get home."

Jake and Bobby said goodbye to Santa and started to run as fast as they could. Back through the wood they went again, looking behind them to make sure that no one was following them.

"Jake, watch out! There are some more snowballs rolling down the hill," shouted Bobby.

At last they could see the tunnel and ran towards it. Once in the tunnel they scrambled as quickly as they could to get to the other end. At last they were back in Jake's back garden.

Bobby said "I hope you enjoyed that Jake and thought it was fun". "Now we must creep quietly up the stairs so that we do not wake anyone up and remember Jake, this is our secret and you must not tell anyone."

When Jake woke up the next morning, he jumped out of bed and went to the window to see if his snowman was still there. Jake noticed that there was no door in the middle of the snowman. Jake was puzzled about this, and as he looked around his bedroom, there was his best friend Bobby on the bed. *Did Bobby come to life last night or was I just dreaming, and did I really go and see Santa?* thought Jake. *I wonder!*

CPSIA information can be obtained
at www.ICGtesting.com
Printed in the USA
LVIC081210111012
3094LVUK00003B